A
Kwanzaa
Fable

▼▼▼▼▼▼▼

Also by

Eric V. Copage

Kwanzaa:
An African Celebration
of Culture and Cooking

Black Pearls

Black Pearls Journal

Black Pearls for Parents

A
KWANZAA
Fable

▲▲▲▲▲▲▲

Eric V. Copage

▼▼▼▼▼▼▼

William Morrow and Company, Inc.
New York

To black people
everywhere
and throughout
all time

Copyright © 1995 by Eric V. Copage

It is the policy of William Morrow and Company, Inc., and its imprints and affiliates, recognizing the importance of preserving what has been written, to print the books we publish on acid-free paper, and we exert our best efforts to that end.

Library of Congress Cataloging-in-Publication Data
Copage, Eric V.
A Kwanzaa fable / by Eric V. Copage
p.   cm.
ISBN 0-688-13968-X (hardcover)
1. Afro-American families—Fiction.   2. Kwanzaa—Fiction.
I. Title.
PS3553. 063315K9   1995
813'. 54—dc20   95-30734
CIP

Printed in the United States of America

First Edition

1 2 3 4 5 6 7 8 9 10

BOOK DESIGN BY NANCY KENMORE

CONTENTS

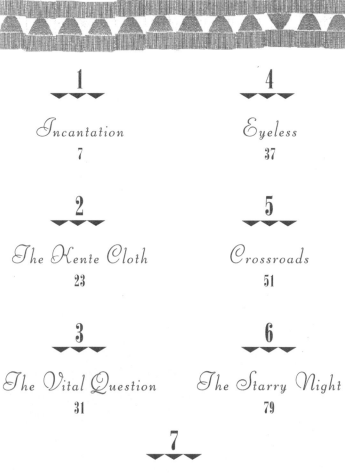

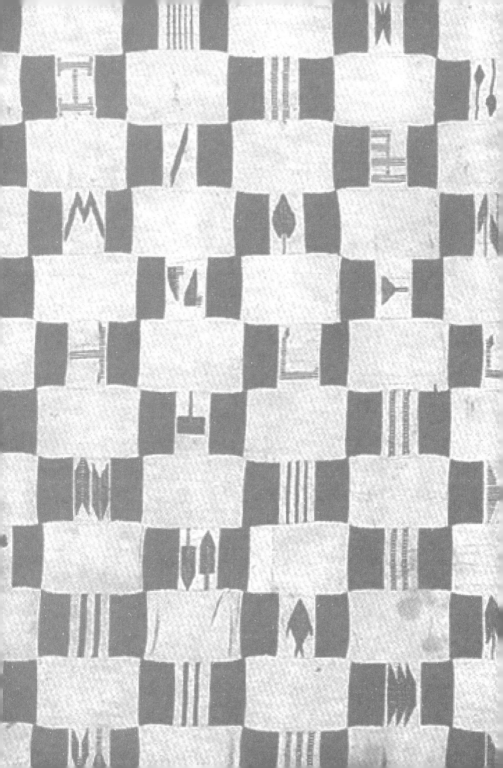

1

Incantation

There are worse places to raise a family than Oakwood, a town a stone's throw from The City. In some parts of this midsize suburb, you can see The City's silhouette— the wedges, spires, and arcs that comprise the web of enterprise where many of Oakwood's residents prosper as lawyers, accountants, and corporate managers. Oakwood neighborhoods that don't offer city vistas offer the cocoon of well-swept streets canopied by shade trees. In spring and summer, when the light is just right, reflections from the leaves of those trees give the houses, ranging from modest multifamily dwellings to mansions, a greenish tinge as well as the usual dancing shadows.

But even in peaceful Oakwood—where squirrels dart across quiet dappled streets—a boy must struggle to become a man. And even in this mostly black town—where talk of African-American heritage, the great African past, and the meanings of kente cloth takes on a prideful, almost magical, air—a black boy needs guidance on his quest to becoming a black man.

And so it was with thirteen-year-old Jordan Garrison. On this hot but mercifully dry Saturday afternoon in late August, he sat on the front-porch steps of the modest, three-story colonial house he shared with his twin eight-year-old brother, Kenny, and sister, Lisa, their grandmother, and their widowed father. Jordan's legs, which didn't seem half so long last month, were doubled up so that his thighs formed a pontoon for each elbow, with his forearms slanted into an A-frame peaked by his clasped hands, upon which he rested his chin.

Jordan directed his gaze toward the twins, who were standing at a card table draped with a paper tablecloth bordered with a kente-cloth pattern. Taped to the streetward side of the table was a carefully stenciled sign whose bold black letters read: LEMONADE 50 CENTS. COOKIES 10 CENTS EACH.

As recently as last Fourth of July, Jordan had worked the stand with the twins. In fact, he had been on that sidewalk selling refreshments in front of his house every Fourth of July since he was five years old. It was the perfect spot, with the Independence Day parade ending about a block from the Garrisons' house. With his father's encouragement and help, Jordan had catered to the parched throngs. As he became older, he took on his father's role—pouring the lemonade, counting the change—while the twins took on Jordan's role of handing drinks and cookies to customers, receiving their money, and giving them change.

After the lemonade sold out, and it sold out every Fourth of July, Jordan and the twins had a profit of twenty to thirty dollars—a king's ransom for a child. They would open the stand on occasion throughout the summer, even though the absence of traffic on their street meant that without a parade, business was far from brisk.

As a teenager, however, Jordan—who had just turned thirteen the previous December—felt that he had outgrown selling lemonade. At the end of the day on last Fourth of July, he decided he would no longer man the stand. The Fourth was one thing; but the idea of a teenager working a lemonade stand when there was obviously more fun than profit involved was totally out of the question. As Jordan watched his siblings chatting with a couple of their friends, he began to cast his mind over the prospects for the coming school year. He would be starting a new school, high school, and as a ninth-grader would be on the school's lowest rung. While he was proud of graduating to this new school, he was also aware of his impending loss of status. He felt as if he were being sent back to the end of the line.

"Jordan! Jordan!" The sharp demand of the voice was distinct. Jordan snapped out of his thoughts and turned in the direction of the voice. His father—a muscular forty-year-old whose squarish face was haloed by short-cropped black hair—rippled into Jordan's consciousness.

"Jordan! Didn't you hear me call you!? Go help your brother and sister pack up. I need all of you to lend a hand with dinner."

Jordan rose from his perch and began to walk over to Lisa and Kenny, who had said good-bye to their friends.

Kenny had used a different language for each friend; *adios, au revoir, ciao, auf Wiedersehen.* By the time Jordan reached the twins, they had started to make a mess out of dismantling the lemonade stand.

Gripping the thermos with both hands, Kenny staggered from side to side, struggling with the enormous container, which was still full of lemonade. Lisa was trying to peel the sign from the table.

"Need any help, Kenny?" Jordan asked his brother.

"No, thanks," said Kenny, who had put down the thermos and was rubbing the pain from his hands.

"Be careful," cautioned Jordan. "You don't want to hurt yourself."

Jordan freed the handmade sign and gave it to Lisa to carry. Then he folded up the table, stuck it under one arm, and caught up with his brother.

"Here, let me help you," said Jordan, grabbing one of the handles of the thermos. Lisa started to protest in her usual quiet voice. Everyone always told Lisa to speak up, but she rarely talked above a whisper. How come Jordan was helping Kenny and not her? But Jordan didn't care to humor her or Kenny. He took the sign between his teeth, put the whole thermos under his free arm, and left the twins behind as he quickly walked back to the house.

Jordan had more important things to think about than Kenny and Lisa—his father's expectations for him, for starters. Throughout Jordan's life, his father had emphasized excellence. He did so less through lectures than with a couple of well-chosen words and very firm action: bad test, no sports that weekend; teacher reports inattentiveness in class, no television. As soon as Jordan learned to read, his father began making up lists for him of things that would "assure success." Items like "Scan your work for the most difficult parts"—"go over your work after it's finished"—would appear time and time again on his father's lists. Mr. Garrison would encourage his son to read these lists before doing his homework assignments, practicing piano, or starting any other activity.

Jordan's bookshelf groaned with soccer, T-ball, softball, and basketball trophies that he had accumulated since kindergarten, playing in the town's various leagues. And he was popular at school. This abundance was as much a testament to his sterling academic work as it was to his physical strength and good nature, for his father would not have let him do any extracurricular activities if he hadn't kept up his grades.

But Jordan's father wasn't only a stern taskmaster; it was he who cheered loudest at his son's sports events. At a win, Mr. Garrison gave enthusiastic high fives; at a loss, a discreet hug or rub on the shoulder that said, "You'll always be a winner to *me*." If Jordan was having a hard time with homework, his father would work patiently with him, guiding his son through the lesson, calmly helping him to look at a problem first this way, then that way, and then another way as a means of helping the boy to find the right answer for himself.

Since Jordan's thirteenth birthday, however, something in the Garrison household had changed. The type of conversations with Dad that used to be casual and easy now almost always deteriorated into harangues about "becoming a man." His father would repeat certain words and phrases in these lectures. It was as if Mr. Garrison believed he could conjure this "man" out of his son with the repetition of the right series of words.

As Jordan entered through the back door into the kitchen, the cool polyphony of jazz billowed from the kitchen radio and a wonderful smell hung in the air: Mr. Garrison was making jambalaya for dinner. Lisa and Kenny raced in and began to bang around as they made successive trips to the cupboard for plates, silverware, and glasses to set on the dining room table. Jordan ran his hands under the faucet and began to wash, shred, and dry lettuce for the salad, then put it in the wooden salad bowl. Jordan's father noticed that not all the leaves were pulled from the head, and that the lettuce was still very damp.

"Son, I'd like you to pull *all* the leaves off the head of lettuce, then dry them *completely*," Mr. Garrison said pleasantly, but firmly. "Now, take it back and do it again."

Jordan dumped the lettuce in the dish towel with a violent shake, then started ripping the remaining leaves from the head. He didn't understand the big deal. The salad was going to be wet with dressing eventually and that wouldn't hurt anybody. But he didn't raise those points with his father. To do so, Jordan knew, would be to risk getting another lecture. And he had been receiving too many of those lately.

As Jordan patted the leaves dry, he heard his father ask, "Are you about through with that lettuce?" Jordan grunted, hoping that was enough of a response to satisfy his father.

"Jordan, I asked you a question."

Just then there was the familiar sound of tires over the asphalt driveway. "Grandma's home," sang out Kenny, who had finished setting everything on the table. Jordan was glad he had been given a reprieve. A trim woman, looking casually stylish in a blue-and-white-checkered gingham dress, stepped through the back doorway, and was immediately hugged by her two youngest grandchildren.

Jordan's grandmother was a very sprightly sixty-two-year-old. Part of her youthful appearance came from her eyes. Like a toddler's eyes aglow at a sugary feast, Grandma looked at the world with her eyes opened wide, as if by some force of will she could pull all the things and sensations of life into her and make them part of her. Grandma's husband had died before Jordan was born, and although she dated and had lots of friends, she focused her energies on being the female figure in the household and helping her son raise the children.

Grandma scanned the countertop where Mr. Garrison had been fixing dinner, the surface neatly arranged with a host of measuring spoons and cups.

"You just won't give up using those things, will you, son," Grandma said, picking up one of the cups in mock exasperation. She eyeballed the dinner in progress, which was bubbling in a stockpot on the stove, tasted a little with a wooden spoon, and closed her eyes to appraise it. She glanced at her son, who was busy with his back to her in another part of the kitchen, then quickly used her fingers to put two pinches of cayenne pepper into the pot. She tasted it again, closed her eyes, and smiled.

Grandma had been living with the family since the death of Jordan's mother from a brain tumor shortly after the twins' birth. Jordan's mother had always been one to place a flower strategically, or decorate a mantel with a piece of cloth. Even when Jordan's father was struggling to get his public relations firm on its feet and there wasn't a dime to spare, Jordan's mother had found a way to brighten everything around them. Now it was Grandma who remembered to add the spot or two of radiance to their house.

"We've finished setting the table," Lisa announced to her father when he turned his attention back to the stove. "May we watch TV?"

"First, I'd like you both to finish those arithmetic problems I gave you. There are only five of them."

"But, Dad," Kenny whined, "a show on *Africa* is about to come on!"

"The most *African* thing you can do right now is to tackle those problems. Then, if there's time, you can watch whatever show you want until dinner is on the table."

Grandma studied Jordan's face. "Looks like your father has been giving you a hard time again," she whispered.

"I wouldn't call it a hard time," Mr. Garrison interrupted. Turning to his son, he said, "Look, Jordan, you're at an age where I don't need to sugarcoat the truth for you. Life can be good, yes, and it can be wondrous. But life is also full of struggle; it is also full of obstacles. When I was your age, my father told me something I never forgot...."

Blah, blah, blah, Jordan thought. He had heard this speech so many times over the past nine months, he practically had it memorized. He could even quote the next lines, which ran through his head silently before his father spoke them: *Everybody chooses weapons when dealing with the difficulties of life, and the choice of weapons determines the distinction with which you meet your trials. You can arm yourself with ignorance, indolence, and pessimism—or with wisdom, discipline, and hope....*

What puzzled Jordan was why his father was wearing out his words of wisdom, and especially, why now? There was also a hint of anxiety in his father's voice when he launched into this subject. Jordan resented the anxiety more than the words themselves. To Jordan, who had always done well in school, his father seemed to be saying, "I don't believe in you!"

A couple of hours after the jambalaya and Grandma's special peach cobbler dessert were just tasty memories, Lisa and Kenny went up to prepare for bed. Jordan's father followed to tuck them in. As Jordan climbed the stairs to his bedroom a few minutes later, he heard his father finishing Lisa and Kenny's special prayers with the coda: "I'll see you in *your* dreams, my chocolate prince and princess. And you'll be in *my* dreams. I love you both very much. Good night." Jordan remembered when he was their age, his father would say his good-nights to him in the same way. Even when Mr. Garrison was working late or away on a business trip as he frequently was, he would call and end the conversation with "I'll see you in *your* dreams, my chocolate prince. And you'll be in *my* dreams. I love you very much. Good night."

Jordan had been in his room for only about twenty minutes listening to music when he thought he heard a commotion in the house. The music was so loud through his headphones that he wasn't sure. Wandering downstairs, he went into the dining room, where he was soon joined by his sister and brother, the three gaping at what they saw. The room looked as if it had been in a minor riot. A chair was overturned and there was a broken glass tumbler and a cracked plate on the floor. Grandma was sobbing, cradling Dad's head in her lap. Dad's lips were lightly parted, his breathing shallow, his complexion waxen.

"Your father's had a heart attack," Grandma said. In the panic beginning to envelope Jordan, he heard a caterwauling ambulance. "I'm going with him to the hospital," his grandmother continued. "I'll call you as soon as we get there."

The ambulance screeched to a halt in front of the house as Jordan ran to open the front door. The legs of a gurney were snapped into place as the ambulance attendants pitched quick questions to Grandma about the victim's condition. They ran an IV line into Mr. Garrison's arm and put an oxygen mask over his face. Jordan caught a glimpse of his father and saw something he'd never seen before in that face: fear. In a blur, the gurney was whisked out the front door.

"Pray for your father," Grandma said to Jordan, Lisa, and Kenny as she hurried along behind the attendants making their way back to the ambulance.

Grandma caught up to the gurney, bent over it, and spoke to her son low and fast. To Jordan, it sounded like a rush of water over rocks, but it was Grandma, repeating something over and over and over again, a torrent of words, like an incantation.

Jordan tried to understand what Grandma was saying, but could seize upon only one thing, the repetition of one word. After the screeching of the ambulance had subsided into eerie silence, Jordan was left with the reverberation of that one word in his ears, the word his grandmother had repeated like a charm.

Hours after the ambulance had left, the word's ghostly echo still rang. Jordan closed his eyes and silently mouthed the word to himself.

And the word Jordan mouthed was *love*.

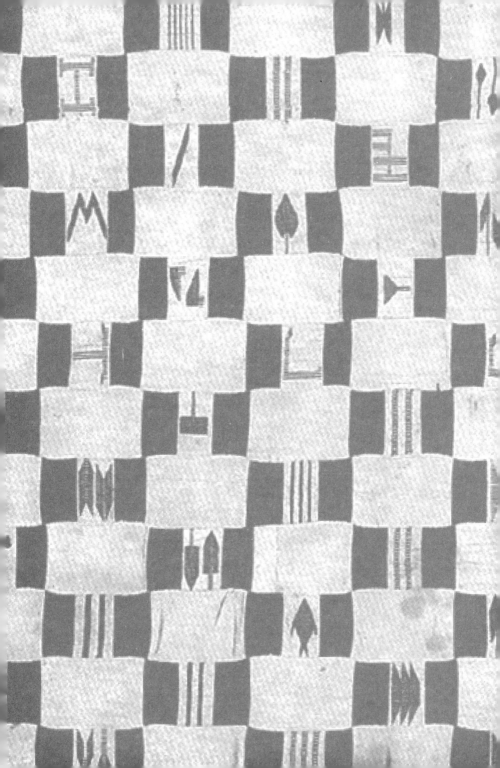

2

▲▲▲▲▲▲▲▲

The Kente

Cloth

▼▼▼▼▼▼▼▼

Jordan couldn't remember the last time he had cried. As a five-year-old, he didn't know what had hit him when his mother passed away. His father explained it by saying that Mommy loved him and his brother and sister very much, but God had called her back. God had called her home. Mommy was happy, Dad had said. She was a brown angel. She was one of the twinkling stars at night. Jordan had no tears back then, just confusion. Why had God called her back? Why had He taken her away from him and his infant brother and sister?

But now, standing next to his father's open grave on this hot, overcast day in early September—the air a damp attack to his forehead, his armpits, the nape of his neck, his back—Jordan felt his knees buckling from the numbness of grief and great sobs erupting from his chest.

He stood next to his grandmother, who wrapped her arms around Lisa and Kenny. Jordan felt the warmth of his grandmother's shoulder against his, and an increasing press of flesh as his relatives, his father's friends, his grandmother's friends, his sister and brother's friends and their parents, his friends and their parents, and teachers and neighbors surrounded his family and offered their condolences. Yet, though Jordan was embraced from all sides, he felt alone. He felt as if he had crossed some threshold, or, more accurately, had been delivered blindfolded to some threshold that he was afraid to cross.

A pair of hands, heavy with silver rings, clasped Jordan's hand and guided him out from the crowd that tried to comfort him. Jordan recognized those hands instantly; they had given him change for many a candy bar, many an ice cream cone, and many a cupcake ever since he was in elementary school.

"I was so saddened to hear about your father," said Snackman, who owned a corner store in the neighborhood. No one knew for sure how old Snackman was. Because of his beard, which was generously flecked with gray, and the receding tide of salt-and-pepper hair, some people guessed he was in his early fifties. But he carried himself with the energy of a much younger man. Snackman himself was mum on the subject of his age.

Today, at the funeral, Snackman wasn't wearing one of his trademark dashikis, but rather the regulation dark suit and tie. A kente-cloth stole draped his shoulders, though.

Snackman put two comforting hands on Jordan's arms as he faced him and looked into his eyes. "I admired your father very much. As much as I know he is a loss to you, he is also a loss to the neighborhood, a loss to all of us. He told me he had been looking forward to seeing you become a black man," Snackman added.

A black man, Jordan repeated silently to himself. He wished he could figure out what his father and Snackman meant. He thought of the black men he'd grown up with, that he'd seen on the streets, in movies, and on television. He thought of the black men he'd read about in newspapers, magazines, and books. He thought of his father. *Do I have to do anything special to become a black man?* Jordan wondered. *Does it simply happen when I reach a certain age?* he asked himself, and was he about to reach that age? Was it simply having experienced a loss or a deep enough pain? Did he become a black man carrying his father's casket down the church steps? Above all, what *is* a black man? Right now, Jordan didn't feel much like any kind of man at all. He felt little and insignificant, like the shadow of a very small child.

Jordan looked at Snackman again and for the first time really noticed the kente cloth he was wearing. Snackman had a wide assortment of kente cloths—all vibrant with reds, greens, blues, golds, and blacks, all woven of the highest quality silk. As Jordan pondered the cloth, Snackman began to lift the kente stole over his head and carefully hand it to Jordan. There was a deliberateness to his movements, as if he were handing over some sacramental object. But as Jordan watched the cloth arch over Snackman's head and down past his face, he noticed that the colors of *this* kente cloth were dull, and the fabric was dirty and frayed. It even seemed to have a stain or two.

"I know your father would have wanted you to have this," Snackman said, handing Jordan the kente cloth. Jordan was baffled and a little repelled by its shabbiness. "Take care of it," Snackman continued, ignoring the look on Jordan's face. "Keep it near you, always, even if that nearness is only in your heart. Any problems, any problems at all, you feel free to call on me. Or if you just want to talk. Stop by. Remember, we're all in this together."

When Jordan returned home, he threw the kente cloth over the inside doorknob of his bedroom. But that night, after he got into bed and turned out his nightstand lamp, he gazed for a long time at the cloth, trying to figure out why Snackman had given him this tattered old piece of fabric, why his father would have wanted him to have it. Night dulled the cloth's already dull colors, except where it was illuminated by tines of moonlight slicing through Jordan's partially open venetian blinds. Bits of the material's geometric patterns seemed to come alive in the interplay of darkness and light. The kente cloth rippled in the faint breeze, lulling Jordan into a sleep. And in that sleep, Jordan had a dream.

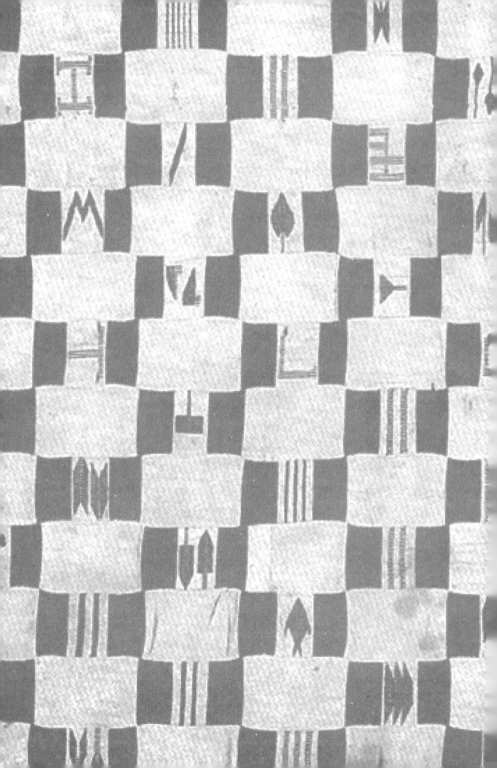

3

▲▲▲▲▲▲▲

The Vital

Question

▼▼▼▼▼▼▼

The sound of Jordan's breathing filled his room, and with every breath he felt himself expanding beyond the boundaries of his skin. He felt himself being lifted higher and higher above his bed. He felt himself misting through the solidity of his ceiling, through the attic, and the roof, and into the warm night air. He felt himself rising through the vapors of the overcast night sky. He saw the lights of his neighborhood, the neighborhoods around it, and eventually, The City itself fanned out below him before it was gradually obscured by clouds. Beyond the sphere of clouds, Jordan soared past tall mountains. He floated over hot desert sands. He drifted through dense, steaming jungles. He sped over windswept prairies of ice. Finally, he came to rest on an immense sun-baked plain of cracked red clay. Before him, under a baobab tree, sat a Ghanaian king on his royal stool. The king was flanked by a hundred of his soldiers, their muskets resting on their shoulders. To the king's immediate right stood his adviser. The adviser approached Jordan:

"You have been brought here to answer three questions. Your life depends on answering these three questions. You have a lifetime to answer these three questions. You may not move from that spot until these questions have been answered." And with that, Jordan heard the clank of metal as the king's soldiers trained their guns upon him.

The adviser continued: "Seven men are standing in a circle in a valley. They wear shackles that have bound them for more than a lifetime. What does the black man do?"

The sun and stars completed their circuit twenty-one times and Jordan had no answer to this first question. He was hot. He was hungry. He was dying of thirst. After another twenty-one circuits of the sun and stars, Jordan was on the edge of despair. But then an answer flashed before his eyes. Jordan wanted to tell the king's adviser, but when he moved his lips to speak, no sound escaped. Jordan looked with pleading eyes as he continued to move his wordless lips. He felt tears of frustration trickle down his cheeks as he struggled to make a sound. The king looked on, unmoved. The soldiers looked on, unmoved. The adviser looked on, unmoved. Finally, Jordan dropped to his knees and tried to scribble the answer with his finger in the bone-hard clay— when he found himself sitting bolt upright in his bed, his sheets moist with sweat, his tongue swollen with thirst, the answer to the vital question gone.

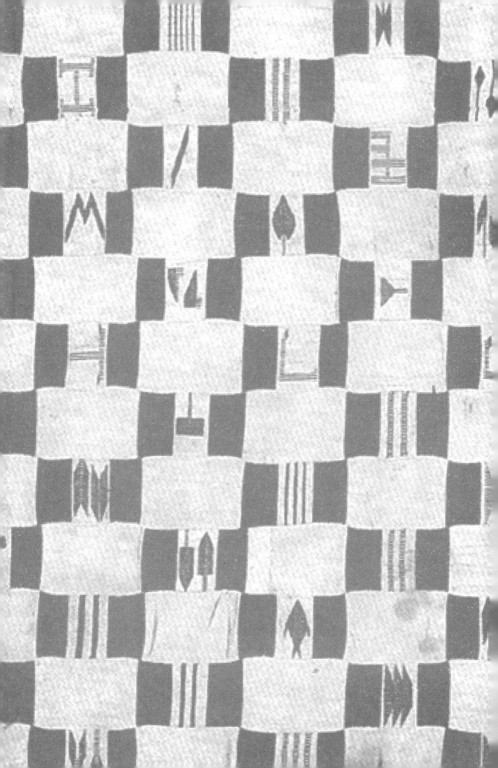

4

▲▲▲▲▲▲▲▲

Eyeless

▼▼▼▼▼▼▼▼

It was with huge relief that Jordan started high school a week later. Amid the confusion and grief of the summer's end, he had forgotten most of his worries about his status at school. In homeroom, Jordan became great friends with J.B.—even though they hadn't really known each other very well in middle school. J.B.—James Barron—was tall for his age. He seemed less to walk than to lope from place to place, with a cool gait. He was not attractive in any conventional way, a discolored front tooth capping a general appearance that made him appear a little sickly. Perhaps to compensate for his homely appearance, J.B. had developed a distinctive personality that impressed many, including his teachers, as charismatic. He had a feline alertness and playfulness; talking with him was like watching a cat batting about a mouse, not out of hunger or malice but for sheer amusement.

J.B. was also somewhat of a troublemaker. He had been mischievous throughout his school career, but in high school he seemed to be using his formidable personality to provoke attention even more than before. Where Jordan and his other friends were at least a little awed and humbled by their new place in the pecking order, J.B. grabbed the opportunity to make his mark on this clean slate. During the first day of school, their homeroom teacher was describing a first job he had had in Hollywood working on a movie set. J.B. raised his hand. "Yes, J.B.," the teacher said. "What you're saying is that you were a flunky," J.B. quipped. There was a tittering around the class as the teacher stammered, "Well, yes, that's essentially correct." There was no hostility in J.B.'s remark, just a simple statement of fact that he alone dared voice. But his boldness did not go unnoticed or unadmired.

Jordan liked the way J.B. and his crowd defied the rules; he began to defy those rules with them. He started ditching classes as they did—checking in at homeroom, then leaving school and returning unnoticed during the lunchtime chaos. When Jordan bagged morning classes, he would ride his bike in one of the town's four large parks, play video games at one of his new friend's houses, or toss pebbles at buses to see the startled, angry expressions of the passengers. Jordan was always accompanied by J.B. on such excursions. Indeed, it was J.B. who seemed to initiate almost everything.

Once, when J.B. suggested missing a whole day of school, Jordan balked. Jordan had already had a couple of close calls with county truant officers (J.B. had, too, but he didn't seem to mind). *What if I should get caught?* Jordan thought. Missing a class or two was on a different scale of misbehavior than missing a whole day. *And what if Grandma found out?*

"Aw, man, don't be soft," J.B. said, trying to goad Jordan into coming with him on his daylong adventure. J.B. and Jordan were standing in the hall as school activity swirled around them, students rushing to first-period class. With J.B. and Jordan were three of their regular running pals. "What, you think you're going to get arrested? You're scared of going to jail? They don't put you in jail for that!" J.B. continued derisively.

"Look," J.B. said, switching tactics, "I'm tight with the truant officers. They won't do anything. They'll just ask you to give them your address so they can send their dumb computer letter to your parents. Don't give them the right address. They don't care."

Jordan was about to defend his position when suddenly, J.B. gave him a look that seemed to preclude further discussion. It was a dismissive sneer that gave Jordan an urge to reverse himself and go with J.B. But before Jordan could get his thoughts together to decide what to say, J.B. had turned on his heels. "Later," he said coldly, and disappeared down the hall followed by the other guys.

The loneliness Jordan felt at that moment was unlike any other loneliness he had ever felt in his life. What made it hurt more was his sense of having been humiliated. Their friends would think of him as a coward, Jordan knew. But most of all, Jordan felt like a child left with baby-sitters while the adults went out to have their fun.

The next day, first thing after homeroom, Jordan pulled J.B. aside. "Let's go to the mall," Jordan suggested.

J.B. thought for a moment, then shook his head and silently shrugged his shoulders, dismissing the idea.

Jordan persisted with an intensity he himself found disconcerting, yet couldn't control. First period was about to start. They had to decide right then if they would escape for the whole day. Jordan enumerated names of stores they could visit, how much fun they could have.

Again there was, for Jordan, a terrible silence, as J.B. mulled over the proposition. "All right," J.B. drawled, then mentioned a couple of things he'd like to do at the mall. The pair slid out of school amid the confusion of changing classes, hopped a bus, and made for the mall.

They went to department stores and tried on leather jackets. Next to shoe stores to admire the newest sneakers. They were kicked out of a sports-equipment shop for playing catch with the merchandise. In the preview section of each of the mall's three music stores, they put on earphones and listened to samples of the latest rap groups. They both mimed performing to the songs, Jordan pretending to be the deejay working the turntables, J.B. doing a precision job of lipsyncing to the records.

Just after noontime, they became hungry and decided to get something to eat. It was a cool, late September day and they needed some hot food before stepping back outside. On their way to a fast-food restaurant, Jordan noticed a jewelry store. In the window were a thick gold pendant and bracelet.

"Hey, check that out," Jordan said. "I wonder how much it costs?"

Each of them tried to open the door, but found it was locked. A sign at eye-level read: RING FOR ENTRY. Inside the store, behind the counter, was a white woman, simply and elegantly dressed in black. A single strand of pearls hung around her neck; her dark hair was tied back in a bun. Her simple black clothes were young and hip, but the half-glasses she peered over made her look like a priggish old schoolteacher. She was talking with another woman, who was wearing a large dark overcoat, and standing on the opposite side of the counter. Jordan figured the woman in the coat to be a customer. But when Jordan pushed the buzzer, the woman behind the counter peered over her reading glasses and mouthed to Jordan and J.B. that the store was closed.

"Follow me," J.B. said. He walked around a corner to a pay phone and called up the jewelry store. In his "whitest" voice, he asked the woman who answered for the store's hours. "So I can come over right now?" J.B. asked. "Good, I'll be right over."

When the saleswoman saw the pair again, her expression told them that she understood that she'd been caught lying. After being buzzed in, Jordan immediately confronted the woman and asked why she had not let them in the first time. But she wasn't listening to him; her attention was riveted on J.B., who was wandering among the display cases in the small shop. He would occasionally ask for the price of this item or that, and the woman would give him an icy reply. Then the doorbell rang again, and the saleswoman buzzed in a mall security guard, a balding middle-aged man. There was an eager seriousness to him that announced he was only too glad to be of service. The guard nodded to the saleswoman, folded his arms, and stood by the door—while directing a menacing glare at Jordan and J.B. Jordan tried to glare back, but J.B. ignored the guard and continued looking around the shop, asking the price of items as they seemed to interest him.

When J.B. finished, he and Jordan left the store. The guard followed them. Stopping to figure out the fastest way to the hamburger stand, Jordan and J.B. turned as the guard stepped up to them and asked if they were lost. This was the last straw for Jordan. He launched into a tirade, exclaiming that they hadn't stolen anything. He felt a prickly sensation pass over his skin; the tips of his ears got hot. The odd thing, Jordan thought to himself while he was railing was that, for some reason, he felt he *had* done something wrong. J.B., on the other hand, simply answered the guard's questions very calmly: No, they weren't lost. Where they were going was none of the guard's business. And if he wanted to call the *real* police, he should go right ahead. Jordan was impressed by how J.B. acted, as if he had every right to be in that mall and there wasn't a hint of his being intimidated. As he thought about it, his admiration for his friend deepened.

On their way home from school, J.B. and Jordan would regularly drop by Snackman's store to pick up a candy bar or bag of corn chips. That day, even with their mall adventure, was no exception. Snackman's store had been located at the corner of Walnut and Forest for as long as anyone could remember. It had no sign. It was just known as the Corner Store, a nondescript brick and concrete storefront with a nondescript wood trim painted a nondescript dark green. But the windows were special. A stenciled sign that read $2.99 BEEF AND CHEESE SANDWICH SPECIAL provided the backdrop for Snackman's weekly displays on black culture—a new display each week. And people would come from miles away to see Snackman's Kwanzaa windows during the holiday season. Even with Kwanzaa a good three months away, people had already begun to look forward to it.

Inside the store, in addition to the chips, cupcakes, and other snacks, in addition to newspapers and magazines, there was the library that Snackman had collected over the years containing books, prints, fabrics, and photographs of the people and places of the African diaspora.

"For three A's, it will be three dollars," Snackman was telling a first-grader who was making a visit to the Corner Store with her mother. Snackman was explaining the possible rewards children could receive from him during report-card time. "But a dollar for an 'A' is nothing compared to what you'll get later in life if you're disciplined and study hard." It was a line every school-aged child in the neighborhood knew by heart, for they were obliged to listen to it if they wanted their prize.

Some parents took a cynical view of Snackman's offer, saying derisively, "That Snackman, he's no fool. He gets his dollar back, and more." Still, for the most part, the adults made a point of buying their Sunday papers, kitchen matches, and sodas at Snackman's store—even though for many the local supermarket was more convenient.

"What's up!" Snackman said to Jordan, as Jordan fished in his pocket for money to buy some chocolate. Jordan shrugged. "I saw the twins at the skating rink yesterday," Snackman continued. "I've never seen two kids have such a good time falling down. They had everyone laughing trying to avoid them. They're getting so big! It seems like just the other day your grandmother was showing me pictures of them getting baptized."

Out of the corner of his eye, Snackman noticed that J.B. and some friends with whom they had linked up were laughing hysterically over in a corner of the store.

"What will it be today, Jordan?" Snackman asked.

"Just these," said Jordan, thrusting out his hand, which contained three dollar bills and a couple of candy bars.

Snackman was about to hand over Jordan's change when

suddenly there was a crash. One of Snackman's many framed, autographed photos had plummeted to the floor, the glass shattering completely. The others in J.B.'s crew looked sheepishly at Snackman, but J.B. was unbowed. "Yo, sorry," he said with a defiant shrug. "Clean it up, J.B.," said Snackman. There was an edge to Snackman's voice that seemed to say, "Don't you even *think* about trifling with me."

After a moment of calculated pause, J.B. complied. With a snarled laugh, "Sure," he said, picking up the frame and tossing it noisily on a nearby counter.

As Jordan followed the snickering crew out of the store, Snackman called to him, "Jordan, you forgot your change." When Jordan reached for it, Snackman held Jordan tightly by the upper arm. "If you run with people like that, be careful of what you do. You and you alone will be held accountable for your actions."

"I know what I'm doing," Jordan snapped, jerking away from Snackman's grasp.

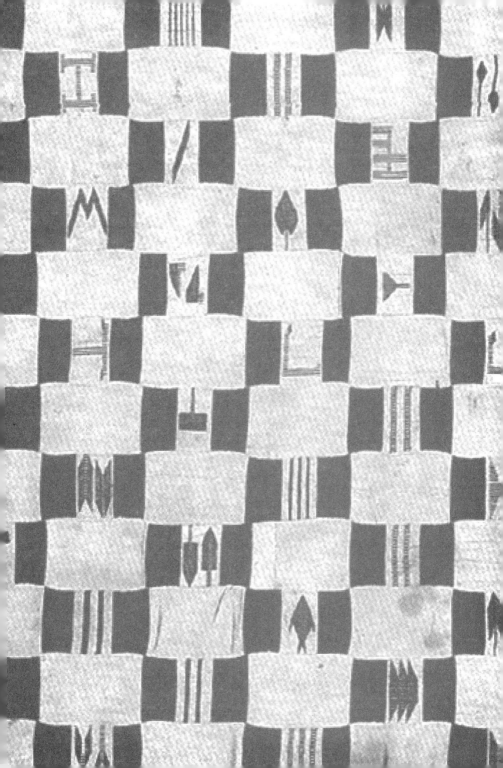

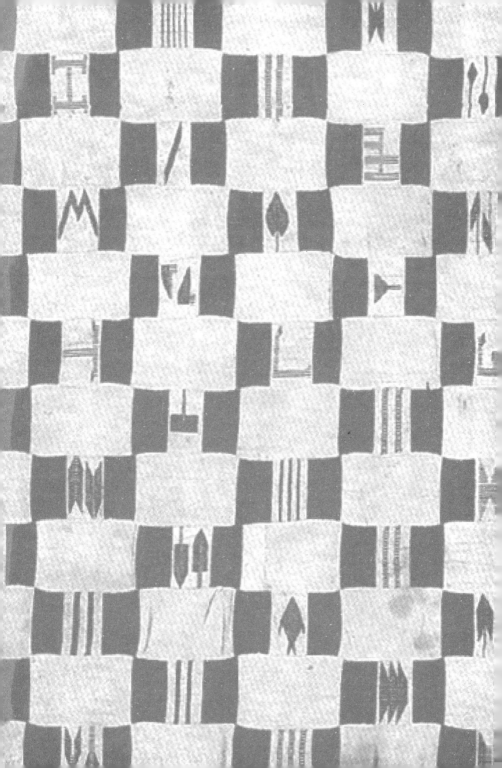

5

▲▲▲▲▲▲▲

Crossroads

▼▼▼▼▼▼▼

An autumnal crispness sheared the early November air. The remaining leaves on Oakwood's tree-canopied streets trembled, flew off their branches, and once fallen, formed a carpet of red, gold, brown, and yellow that rippled in the wind. Rich shadows and the deep golden light of sunrise laid long fingers across the town.

It had been six weeks since Jordan and J.B.'s first mall trip. During those six weeks, they had managed to become the two most popular guys in school.

They were on everyone's party invitation lists, and their lunch table was crowded with admirers and hangers-on.

It was just when the fall party season had really started that Jordan's grandmother told him that she had found part-time work. Since his father's estate wouldn't be settled until the new year, they could use the money.

"Jordan, I'm going to have to work afternoons and evenings, Tuesday through Saturday. So you won't be able to go to parties at night," Grandma said, fussing over the twins as she rushed to prepare them for their school bus. "That also means no hanging out after school."

Jordan's heart sank. He knew that Grandma had been planning to get a job. And he knew that would mean he'd have additional responsibilities. But he hadn't realized that his social life would be quashed entirely.

"You've baby-sat for the twins plenty of times before, so I know you can handle it," said Grandma, checking the twins' backpacks for homework and lunch. "Besides, they're practically old enough now to take care of themselves." She dampened a bit of paper napkin, cleaned the corner of one of Lisa's eyes, then used another corner to wipe Kenny's mouth.

Jordan knew that Grandma had no other choice, yet he still felt put-upon. He had finally become a big deal at school and now, just as parties were getting under way, he would have to baby-sit for the twins every single night.

One Saturday morning, a week after Grandma had started her new job, Jordan was walking around the neighborhood, letting off steam. Soon he found himself standing outside Snackman's store. It was the first time he'd been there in weeks. Under J.B.'s influence, they had completely avoided Snackman after the picture incident. "Who needs that old fool telling me what to do," J.B. had snapped. Jordan was about to move on, when he heard Snackman call to him.

"What's been going on?" Snackman said. While Jordan felt empowered by his new status at school, the things that made him popular were not things he wanted to share with Snackman. He avoided the question and explained in garbled tones that he hadn't been around because he felt uncomfortable about coming by after the incident with the picture.

"Oh, I didn't mind the picture, but I did mind the disrespect," Snackman said. "But I was a teenager once, believe it or not, so—" He punctuated his sentence with a smile. "You and your friends are always welcome here." Then he added with a laugh, "Of course, I'm still not going to take nonsense from you all."

Moments of awkward silence followed as Jordan nervously moved his eyes around the store. He was about to speak. He wanted to talk about his grandmother's new job and how he resented being told to stay home and look after the twins— as if he were a child himself. But he said nothing. Snackman sensed that something was wrong, that Jordan seemed angry at the world.

"What's bothering you?" Snackman asked. Still Jordan wanted to talk, but said nothing. He wanted to tell Snackman about the overwhelming feeling of power he had at school, especially when he was next to J.B. He wanted to say how mad he was at his grandmother—who expected him to accept so many unanticipated responsibilities, without complaint. Finally, Jordan blurted out that he felt his grandmother treated him like a kid.

Snackman let Jordan's resentful words subside, then, leaning over the counter with exaggerated confidentiality, said, "I wasn't always a black man, you know." He peered at Jordan from the corners of his eyes, a smile playing on his lips.

Jordan studied Snackman's face, his kinky hair, dark-brown skin, and thick lips. He wondered if his new friends weren't right after all—maybe Snackman was just a crazy old fool.

For his part, Snackman seemed to be enjoying Jordan's confusion. Snackman pulled the sleeves of his dashiki up to his elbows, raised his arms and hands and rotated them directly in front of Jordan's face, like a magician about to perform a miraculous trick.

"This," Snackman said, glancing at his exposed skin, "is not what makes me a black man." He paused dramatically. "*This* is," he said, tapping his hand to his heart. "And *this*," he said, tapping his hand to his temple. Snackman let his sleeves down and looked, no longer playfully, at Jordan.

"There comes a time in every black person's life when he or she arrives at a crossroads," Snackman said, staring at Jordan to gauge the effect of his words. "There comes a time in black people's lives when they have to decide what *they* mean when they say they are black, when they say that they are of African heritage. When they arrive at that crossroads, most people aren't even aware of it, but that doesn't make it any less real. You, Jordan, are now at that crossroads."

Jordan bristled with anger. It sounded to him like Snackman was challenging his racial pride. He felt an indignation rise from deep within him. After all, Jordan thought, he knew most of the famous black-American leaders of the past—and not just because of black history month. He could quote Malcolm X, and was no stranger to prejudice. He had several T-shirts with pictures of the Motherland on it, and he wore those T-shirts proudly. Why, Jordan could even count to ten in Swahili! "Nobody tells *me* how to be black," Jordan fumed with a vehemence that surprised even himself.

"What you mean is that nobody but you *should* tell you how to be black," Snackman calmly corrected. "You already have thousands of people telling you how to be black. They are on television shows, in magazine and newspaper articles, in movies, in school.

"I'm not telling you how to be black or how black to be," Snackman continued. "I'm not telling you that you are two shades too light or that you are two shades too dark."

He rose from behind the counter and led Jordan to the door. Then, as he shook Jordan's hand good-bye, Snackman said, "I'm simply making an observation: You are at a crossroads. It's a crossroads to which we all come.

"Think about what I said, about coming to this crossroads. We all need guidance when we reach it. In the kente cloth, I have given you a marker. But remember: The menu is not the meal; the reflection not the object reflected; and the symbol not the thing symbolized. And continue to remember," Snackman said, "that my door is always open to you. If you need my help, just call. Anytime. Because we are all in this together."

The basement of the Garrison house was filled with an intoxicating and noxious mixture of fumes from paint and glue. Jordan threw open the door to the backyard and a cold breath of November evening air rushed in, clearing everyone's head. Assembled were Jordan, J.B., and the twins, whose school art project was the source of the fumes. Grandma wouldn't return until much later.

Jordan left the door open a crack, poured a couple of

glasses of soda, and handed one to J.B., who was sitting on a folding chair in front of the washer and dryer.

The twins' school project was laid out on a bench. Their task was to research the traditional meaning of the colors and patterns used in kente-cloth designs. Next, they were to create a design that would express something they wanted to say about themselves, their family, or their culture.

Kenny knew that he was looking for something that spoke about power, like the comic book superheroes he liked; Lisa, with Halloween still on her mind, was thinking of ghosts. And so the twins' designs would look very different as they progressed. But both patterns were to be laced with gold, which Lisa and Kenny had learned represents prosperity, royalty, and the influence of God in human life. Right now they were fighting for who would use the gold. Jordan snapped at them to be quiet and took the gold paint away.

Throughout the afternoon, the twins' big brother had been curt with them, especially when they turned to him for help on their project. When Lisa asked what a certain word in the book she was reading meant, Jordan dismissed her with, "Look it up yourself." When Kenny told Jordan that he and Lisa had borrowed Snackman's kente cloth to copy one of its patterns, Jordan barely listened. Instead, Jordan cut him off and brusquely ordered the kids to "be quiet and finish your projects!" By the time J.B. arrived, Jordan was in a foul mood. And the twins were glumly trying to finish up.

"Man," J.B. whispered, "don't let everybody cramp you, tell you what to do, who to be, where you're at. As long as you let everybody push you around, they're going to push you around some more."

To Jordan, this seemed to make sense.

"Stand up for yourself," J.B. continued. "Stop acting like a child, they'll stop treating you like one." J.B. shrugged, and leaned closer to Jordan. "I wouldn't be a friend if I didn't tell you this, but people are laughing at you behind your back."

J.B. wouldn't say which people, but added, "Listen. In about an hour, some of us are getting together over at Mike's house. Put the twins to bed and swing on by. Your brother and sister won't miss you, and you'll be back before your grandmother comes home. Man, you've got to hang! People are forgetting who you are!"

Jordan thought that a party sounded like a great idea. Besides, during the past weeks that he had been baby-sitting, the evenings had all been so *nothing*. Totally dull. Jordan longed for some excitement; he told Lisa and Kenny to get ready for bed quickly. After they were all brushed, washed, and in their pajamas, Jordan closed their bedroom door, which was usually left open, so that the twins wouldn't hear the back door shut when he left the house. Kenny and Lisa panicked.

"Don't shut our door!" Kenny screamed.

Jordan swung the door open and with great agitation reentered the room. "I have to," Jordan said. "I'm going to listen to the radio and I don't want to keep you up."

"Put on earphones," Lisa implored.

"I don't want to," Jordan said, with no attempt to hide his exasperation.

"But, I'm scared," Lisa persisted.

"Look," Jordan said, impatiently, "there's nothing to be scared of, but if you need some comfort, get one of your dolls and snuggle with it. Really, it will be all right. Now I'm going to shut the door. I want to listen to my music and I don't want to use earphones. You'll be all right. Now go to sleep!" Jordan walked out of the room, firmly shutting the door behind him. He thought he had forgotten something, but he couldn't figure out what it was.

As soon as he arrived at Mike's house, Jordan felt his heart skip a beat. He had forgotten to say the family's special prayers for his brother and sister. He couldn't remember a time when that had happened before. His father had said those nighttime prayers to Jordan without fail until he was at least ten years old. Dad's prayer was, "Dear God—thank you for giving my son, Jordan, a strong mind and a strong, healthy body. Thank you for making him successful in everything he does. Amen." Every night Jordan had baby-sat he remembered to say the "thank you for giving my brother, Kenny, and sister Lisa, strong minds..." And he knew Grandma *never* forgot the twins' special prayers. His little sister and brother must have been so panicked when he shut their door that they forgot to remind him. At the threshold of Mike's house, Jordan flirted with the idea of going back home. But the twins were probably asleep by now, he reasoned. No matter. It would be all right, he reassured himself, and plunged into the party.

Well, it really wasn't a party. It was just a bunch of kids standing around gawking. Or giggling. The living room was divided, with ten girls or so on one side, and about the same number of boys on the other, all trying to figure out their first moves. J.B. soon broke the ice with a joke, then cranked up the music, and the party was off and running.

After a couple of hours, Jordan decided he'd better head back to his house. He didn't want to cut it too close. When he got home, he looked at the clock. Ten-thirty, a cool half hour before Grandma usually arrived. Jordan buttered a slice of bread, poured himself a glass of milk, and made his way toward the stairs. Things had gone so smoothly, he thought, that perhaps he would make a regular habit of sneaking out while his brother and sister were asleep. As he climbed the stairs, he smelled something. At first, he thought it was a bit of toast that had gotten stuck in the toaster, then he realized he hadn't toasted his bread. He looked up and saw a thin haze of smoke coming from under the door to the twins' room. He raced up the stairs and opened the door to their room, which was thick with smoke. Kenny's electric blanket had shorted. While there were no flames, the hot wires from the blanket had begun to burn into the mattress. Jordan could see the circle of orange embers from which the smoke rose.

He rushed into the room and carried the twins out into the hall. They were groggy from the smoke and sleep, but definitely alive. Both started to cry. Jordan had told his little brother not to plug in the old electric blanket. As Jordan guided his staggering brother and sister down the stairs, Kenny was saying, "I'm sorry," over and over again. Jordan held Kenny's hand tight to reassure him and told both of them to put on their coats over their pajamas and wait for him on the front porch. He then called the fire department, and tried to reach his grandmother at her job, but she had already left.

When Jordan rushed back to the front door, he saw that Lisa was still inside, struggling to put on her coat. She was having trouble putting one of her hands through her sleeve;

her hand, balled into a fist, clutched the kente cloth Snack-man had given Jordan at his father's funeral. It was singed and reeked of smoke. Jordan gently pried the fabric from his sister's hand and tossed it back into the house, in a corner of the entrance hallway. Then he helped his sister put on her coat and ushered her into the cold, where they all waited for the firemen to arrive.

"I heard you were a hero last night," said Snackman the next day, raising his hand to give Jordan "five." It was Saturday morning and Snackman had been sweeping the sidewalk in front of his store when he saw Jordan and J.B. walk by. The two were so involved in conversation that Snackman had taken them by surprise. They both fidgeted with discomfort—Jordan, because he knew that not only was he not a hero but was almost the cause of his brother and sister's death—J.B., because he hated to suffer listening to "that crazy old fool" Snackman.

Jordan unenthusiastically extended his hand, face up, to receive Snackman's "five" and responded that he was not really a hero. "Everyone in the family was just lucky last night."

"Well, your grandmother thought that it was more than good luck," Snackman said. Jordan remembered that conversation with Grandma the night before, how she had come home to find Jordan with the twins safely outside, the ambulance and fire truck already there. Jordan remembered how relieved his grandmother was that everybody was alive and safe. (It turned out that Kenny had been cold, and, after calling for Jordan many times, plugged in the old electric blanket even though he knew he wasn't supposed to. Jordan told his grandmother that he was in the basement, not out of the house, and that was why he hadn't heard Kenny calling for an extra blanket.)

Now Snackman gave Jordan a friendly, but steady gaze for a quiet moment. The teenager felt an uncomfortable itching in his throat. "Anyway," Snackman said, at last, "it's a good thing you were there and woke them up in time." Then he invited the boys into his store for a free juice or soda.

"Come on, it'll be on me. Think of it as a reward," Snackman said.

J.B., his defenses down after seeing that Snackman was not going to pick up where their last conversation left off, explained that they had to catch a bus to the city, where they were going to check out sound equipment for the rap group they were planning to form. The twins had spent the night in the hospital, just for observation. Jordan's grandmother would take a day off now to make sure they rested at home. So Jordan was free to join J.B. for the whole day.

"Well, come on inside, grab a drink and take it with you,"

Snackman insisted. "About when will the bus arrive?"

"In about twenty-five minutes," Jordan said.

"Well then, you have plenty of time. It's only a five-minute walk to the bus stop. Come on in," said Snackman, leading the way.

Inside the shop, Snackman handed them the apple juice and grape soda they had requested. "Tell me about this group. Do you have a name?"

"Not yet, but we're working on it. Jordan wants to be the deejay. I like to rap, and we thought we might get another rapper, possibly a girl." J.B. said.

"I've already got a pretty good twelve-inch collection and one turntable," Jordan volunteered. "I just need to get another and a sound system. There are a couple of stores in the city that are supposed to have pretty good deals."

"And once you find out how much it costs, where are you going to get the money?" Snackman asked.

Jordan looked baffled. In the initial rush of wanting to start a group, he had totally overlooked that basic question. "W—Well," he stuttered, "I—I have some savings." But even as he said it, he knew that the meager amount he had wouldn't begin to cover the cost of the equipment he needed.

"Listen," Snackman said, reading Jordan's look. "If you need work, we should talk. I don't need help around the store right now, but if you're good with a lawnmower, maybe we can work out something else. You know," Snackman mused out loud, picking up steam, "I don't suppose there's any harm in letting a thirteen-year-old get a little entrepreneurial experience. I own a two-family house on Walnut Street. Since it's near Thanksgiving, you can rake the remaining leaves, clean gutters, and help me with the odd maintenance that needs to be done. Come spring, there'll be grass in need of mowing, weeds to pull, hedges to trim. I can pay you... six dollars an hour for a few hours over the weekend. That's more than minimum wage. In a month, you can save at least fifty dollars, which can help you launch your music career."

Upon hearing that, J.B. laughed out loud. "Man, that's chump change." He turned to Jordan. "I told you Snackman is crazy!"

Before Snackman could respond, a young woman walked into the store. As soon as she saw Snackman, she beamed, "How you doing, Snackman?" giving him a kiss on the cheek. She chatted about having a lot of errands to do that day, but quickly got to the reason of her visit. Leaning close to Snackman, she spoke in a murmur as she drew a fat envelope from her overcoat. J.B. beckoned Jordan to look at a picture in a magazine, which they gazed at blindly, focusing their attention instead on the woman, trying to hear her words.

She explained that her grandaunt, one of Snackman's tenants, wasn't able to get to the bank for a money order to mail in. But because the rent was due the next day, she had asked her grandniece to bring it in cash. It was a good opportunity, the young woman said, for a quick visit; she still had the first Snackman dollar she got for her first "A" in school.

After the woman left, Jordan said to Snackman, "I never knew before today that you're a landlord." Snackman beamed, putting the envelope in a drawer under the counter. "It was a good investment," he said proudly, and then glanced at J.B., but directed his comment to Jordan. "You should never be afraid to start out small. It helped me get to where I am today."

J.B. cracked up. "Snackman, you own a two-bit candy store and a small, old, two-family house—*biiig* deal."

Snackman just shook his head. "The trouble is, J.B., it's your *thinking* that's small."

J.B. joked, "Hey, money's cool. Just don't act like no Donald Trump."

The phone rang and Snackman picked it up. After a couple of seconds, he put the caller on hold. "If anyone comes in, tell them I'll be right back," Snackman said, before disappearing into the basement.

J.B. leaned over to Jordan and pointed with his chin in the direction of the envelope.

"I've got the answer to your money worries, Jordan." Jordan couldn't believe J.B. was talking about robbing Snackman. After his narrow escape from the night before, Jordan felt he had courted enough danger for the time being. And Snackman was his friend. And he knew it was just plain wrong. J.B. broke into a smile and seemed to be able to read Jordan's thoughts in his face.

"I wouldn't steer you wrong," J.B. said reassuringly. "There are no lives at stake here. It's just some easy cash that will help you get where you want to go."

Jordan felt his fear of catastrophe lessen, but a solid wall of conscience kept him from seriously entertaining the idea.

J.B. seemed to intuit his partial victory. "Listen," J.B. whispered intently, keeping up his momentum. "Snackman just lives off black people the way white people do. What's the big deal? That he gives you a buck for your 'good' grades? Those lame black-pride displays he puts in his windows?"

Jordan had never considered this before, but his friend seemed to have thought it all out. J.B. took another swig of his soda, and made a disdainful face. "He's just a crazy old man—he'll probably never even miss it."

Clearly, Jordan thought, this was a test. J.B. could just as easily steal the money himself, but he was prodding Jordan to take it.

"Snackman trusts you, Jordan," J.B. pointed out. "He'll never even come looking in *your* direction.

"Or maybe," J.B. continued, "you just don't have the guts."

He chugged his remaining soda and crushed the can. "Maybe I had you all wrong. Maybe you really are still a kid." He said no more, just rotated the crushed soda can in his hand and stared at Jordan.

"OK," Jordan said.

J.B. smiled.

Snackman returned to the phone, gave his caller some information, and hung up. The boys said their good-byes to Snackman and headed off to the bus stop. But they had decided that they would only pretend to get on the bus. J.B. would go right home and stay there. Then Jordan would sneak into the Corner Store when Snackman was again in the basement—and take the money from the drawer. That was the plan.

Later that day, the Garrisons were in the kitchen. The twins had asked to put a new message on the answering machine and Grandma and Jordan were trying to help them. But every time Jordan pointed his finger meaning "Start now!" Lisa became tongue-tied, no matter how well she had rehearsed it. And she was not helped by Kenny, who playfully switched words in his part of the greeting—changing *residence* to *home* to *domicile*.

The doorbell rang and Jordan volunteered to get it. When he opened the front door, he found J.B. standing there.

"Well? Did you get the money?" J.B. asked.

Jordan shushed J.B., but J.B. persisted.

"Yeah, yeah," Jordan finally said. "Now get out of here. It's a bad time," and started to shut the door.

J.B. put his foot out, where it met the closing door with a quiet thump. "So where is it?" J.B. said.

"Who is it, Jordan?" Grandma called out from the kitchen.

Jordan ignored her and spoke to J.B. from the narrow opening between the door and the doorframe. "Upstairs," he answered in a raspy whisper. "I hid it."

J.B. smiled and withdrew his foot.

The next day was Sunday, and Jordan went to church with Grandma, Kenny, and Lisa. In the midst of all the huddled figures scurrying down the church steps to escape the late-November chill, there was one figure that did not move. When Jordan recognized the figure as J.B., he averted his eyes and quickened his step.

"Isn't that your friend J.B.?" Jordan's grandmother asked.

"Yeah," Jordan replied crossly, and turned away from him as much as possible without being too obvious. J.B. simply followed his friend with his eyes and smiled.

That Monday at noon, Jordan sat at the corner of a lunch table by himself. But soon he was joined by J.B., who gave him a robust slap on the back before sliding down next to him.

"Which turntable are you going to buy?" he asked Jordan. By now, they were also joined by three other boys: one was light-skinned and heavyset with reddish hair; one was gaunt, tall, and dark; and the third, a boy of medium color and build who had a shaved head.

"I'm not so sure that I am going to buy one," Jordan said.

J.B. looked surprised. "Why not, that's why you took the money isn't it?" His eyes narrowed. "You *did* take the money, didn't you?"

"Yes, I did," Jordan said curtly. "I just don't know what I want to buy with it."

"What money are you talking about?" the heavyset boy with reddish hair asked the newcomers at the table. J.B. filled everybody in.

"How much did you get?" the teen with the shaved head asked.

"Five hundred dollars," J.B. volunteered for Jordan.

"Man, that's a good take," the tall, dark boy said with admiration.

"Yeah, but homey here was scared stiff. He almost chickened out," J.B. said.

"I wasn't scared, and I didn't chicken out," Jordan said, and he found himself bragging about how clever and cunning the theft had been.

Shortly after the last-period late bell rang, Jordan was summoned to the principal's office. Mr. Southgate was a large man. A former college football star, he was, like so many men of that build, beginning to become merely bulky in his middle age. Although he carried himself with the stern self-importance of the most exacting bureaucrat, he was a great champion on behalf of his students, and used his authoritative style and grant-writing talents to get all sorts of extra programs and equipment for his school. Southgate looked at Jordan for a moment, as if sizing him up, and then said, "There's been a robbery." Jordan felt his heart pound. "The owner of the Corner Store came to my office this morning to report a theft of five hundred dollars. Do you know anything about this?"

Jordan shook his head. The principal went on to say that three other students had been individually questioned; each claimed that Jordan had bragged at lunch that he had stolen the money.

Jordan stuttered, "I—I didn't do it."

Mr. Southgate was silent for a moment. "In all likelihood, this will go to the police. You know, of course, that you are in serious trouble. You'll be tried as a juvenile offender. You'll certainly be expelled from this school." He paused, then told Jordan that it was better to cooperate, even if they still wouldn't be able to avoid most of the unpleasantness.

Jordan now shouted out, "But I didn't do it!"

The principal looked at him. "Do you remember telling three students of this school that you did?"

Jordan looked down.

Mr. Southgate informed Jordan that he had no choice but to suspend him until the matter was resolved, adding that he had called Jordan's grandmother, who was on her way to school.

Jordan was numb. Mr. Southgate rose from his desk and turned toward the door. Snackman stood there, looking at Jordan. Snackman's face was impassive—like an African ceremonial mask.

The principal left the room and shut the door. Now, it was only Jordan and Snackman in the room.

"I didn't do it, Snackman!"

Snackman studied him for a while. "Don't you think that it's curious that three kids—friends of yours—said you claimed you *did* do it?" Feeling miserable and ashamed, Jordan explained that he was just trying to impress them.

Snackman slowly shook his head. "Is that what your friends find impressive? Stealing? These are not the values of black culture."

Jordan was in a cold sweat. He thought of how he was disgracing the memory of his father and mother. There was a sharp knock at the door and Jordan's grandmother swung it wide, standing in the doorway.

"Is this true what I hear, that you have been stealing! And from Snackman, yet!" Her eyes were on fire. She stomped over to Jordan, grabbed his arm, and was about to pull him to his feet so that she could confront him face-to-face. But then Snackman caught her eye and made a subtle gesture with his hands, indicating that he and Jordan were in the middle of something.

Grandma released Jordan's arm. In a tone more plaintive than angry, she asked, "Is this true, baby?"

No one spoke for a long time. Finally Snackman spoke to Jordan's grandmother. "Look, I don't really believe he stole this money." Then he looked at Jordan. "It just isn't like you. But what I really don't understand is, why you'd *brag* that you were a thief?"

"It was a big deal with J.B.," Jordan explained. "J.B. tried to talk me into stealing the money, but I couldn't do it."

Jordan was sunk. He winced as he remembered what Snackman had told him at the store: *If you run with people like that, be careful of what you do. You and you alone will be held accountable for your actions.*

Jordan was about to ask if Snackman believed him, when the principal reentered. Grandma asked Mr. Southgate what the next move would be. Jordan's head sank. "I'll wait until tomorrow before I call the police," Mr. Southgate said.

"I don't think the police will be necessary," Snackman said. "I believe Jordan is innocent."

The principal frowned. "You'd best talk to the police if you ever expect to see that five hundred dollars again. The sooner, the better. Now is the time to stop him before it is too late. Before stealing becomes a habit."

Snackman considered his words. "You have a point," he said, "but I simply don't believe Jordan did it."

Snackman turned to Jordan and spoke forcefully. "OK, Jordan, you say you are innocent. I believe you. But now, you have to prove it to all of us."

Jordan had never imagined that J.B. would steal the money if he didn't. And he knew J.B. would never admit to the theft. Jordan was scared. He had to prove his own innocence, but hadn't the slightest idea how.

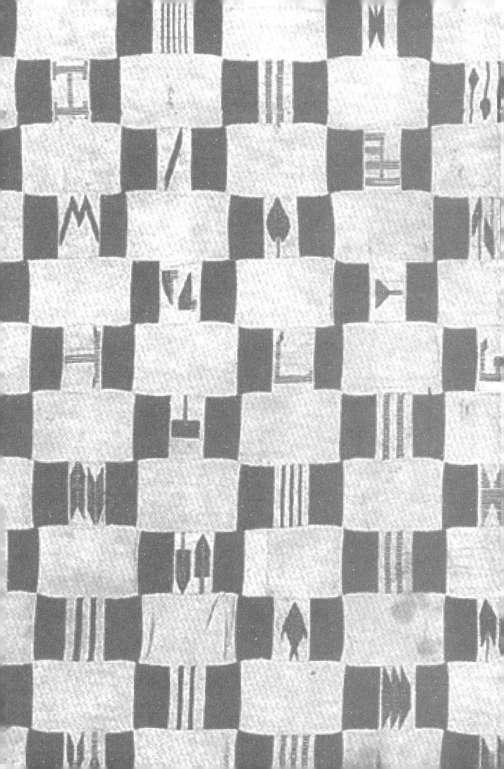

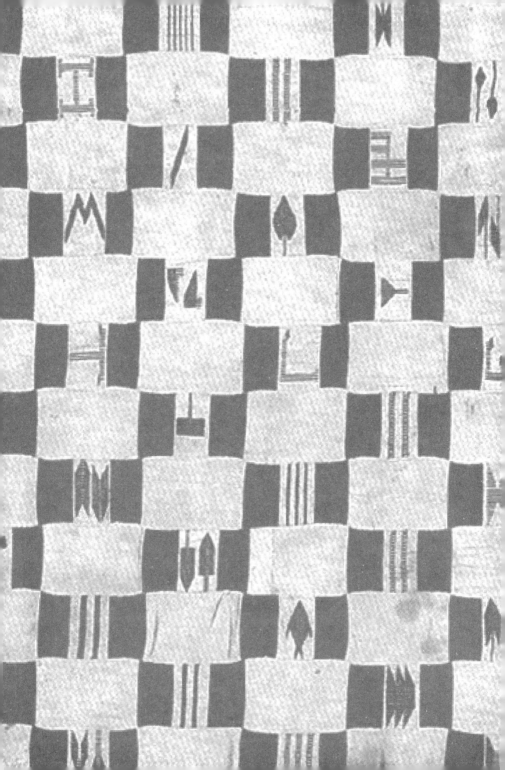

6

▲▲▲▲▲▲▲

The Starry

Night

▼▼▼▼▼▼▼

In his bedroom that evening, Jordan heard the prattle of a television show that Lisa and Kenny were watching, and the clanking of pots and spoons as Grandma cooked dinner. Jordan shut the door to his room and sat at his desk. He absentmindedly rubbed between his fingers the now-singed kente cloth Snackman had given him at his father's funeral. As he rubbed the cloth, his mind moved beyond the turbulence of his thoughts. He felt himself misting through the solidity of his room and into the inky blackness of the starry night. Beyond the sphere of stars and night, Jordan soared past the sphere of tall mountains, the sphere of hot desert sands, the sphere of steaming jungles, and the sphere of windswept prairies of ice.

Finally, Jordan came to rest on an immense sun-baked plain of cracked red clay. Before him, under a baobab tree, sat the Ghanaian king on his royal stool. The king was flanked by a hundred of his soldiers, their muskets resting on their shoulders. To the king's immediate right stood his adviser. The adviser approached Jordan:

"You have been brought here to answer three questions. Your life depends on answering these three questions. You have a lifetime to answer these three questions. You may not move from that spot until these questions have been answered." With that, Jordan heard the clank of metal as the king's soldiers trained their guns upon him.

The adviser continued: "Seven men are standing in a circle in a valley. They wear shackles that have bound them for more than a lifetime. What does the black man do?"

The sun and stars completed their circuit twenty-one times before Jordan had the answer, but once he flashed upon it, words leapt from his lips like sparks from an iron-smith's forge.

"The black man uses his infinite cunning to escape his shackles, then hammers those shackles into seven spears," Jordan replied.

"And what does the black man do with those seven spears?"

"He hurls them in one direction."

"And in what direction does he hurl them?"

"He hurls them toward the North Star."

It was night suddenly and Jordan was alone on the vast, bleak plain. Flashes of lightning near the horizon illuminated the ghostly silhouette of the baobab tree. A moment later, the welcome rumble of thunder reached Jordan's ears. He stretched his hands heavenward and closed his eyes as the first drops of revitalizing rain trickled down his cheeks.

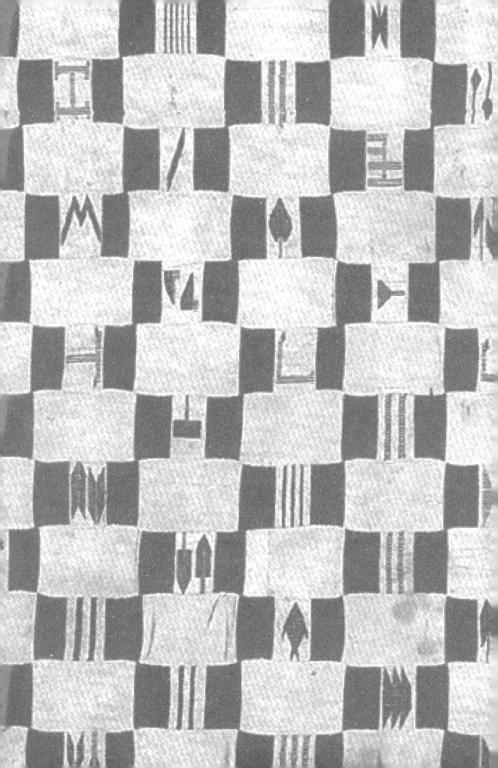

7

Return

The next day, J.B. was in the boys' locker room after his sixth-period gym class. He was joking around with his three friends from the cafeteria. Suddenly, Jordan appeared at the far end of the row of lockers and walked toward the group. J.B. was stunned.

"I thought you had been suspended," said J.B.

"I was," Jordan replied, "but Snackman agreed to drop everything if he got the money back—so I returned his five hundred dollars."

J.B. squinted in disbelief. "You gave him back five hundred dollars?!"

"It was either that or get expelled and end up in who knows what kind of mess," Jordan said matter-of-factly.

J.B. rubbed his chin thoughtfully. He seemed to have trouble putting this together. For the first time, it seemed to Jordan, J.B. was flustered, at a loss for words. "Why'd you end up leaving five hundred dollars behind?" J.B. asked.

"What are you talking about," Jordan said, narrowing his eyes quizzically. "Like I said, I saw five hundred dollars—and I took it."

J.B. thought for a moment, then erupted into low ripples of laughter. "No, man, you could have got a *thousand* bucks! There were still five hundred left over by the time I snuck in." And he dug into his pocket and came out with a wad of bills, which he waved in Jordan's face.

"What?" Jordan asked.

"You must have been nervous or something, because Snackman still had five hundred bucks more in that drawer when I got there. It's too bad you got caught, Jordan." Then he added with a laugh, "You shouldn't have talked so much."

The three friends looked at J.B. in disbelief. When Jordan first told them J.B. had stolen the money, they thought Jordan was lying. They thought it was just a desperate and pathetic ruse by Jordan to get off the hook. They had ragged on Jordan for trying to blame someone else for the theft he himself had bragged about, and were especially disappointed that he should try to blame it on such a good friend. But when Jordan told them they could witness J.B.'s confession from J.B.'s own lips, curiosity got the better of them. They knew Jordan would show up in the locker room after sixth-period gym, and they knew there would be some kind of confrontation. They never expected this.

Now all the boys stood in the narrow aisle of lockers looking at one another, speechless. Finally, the heavyset teen with reddish hair addressed J.B.

"That's messed up, J.B.," he said, a trace of uncertainty in his voice.

"What's messed up?" J.B. shot back, his voice dripping with intimidation.

"Letting Jordan take the rap for what you did," said the tall boy.

None of them would have challenged J.B. individually, but collectively they seemed to find the strength to do it.

"OK," J.B. said after a pause, "I took some of Snackman's money, but so did Jordan. He bragged about it, and he got caught."

"I never stole any money," Jordan told J.B. "Snackman had only five hundred dollars in the drawer, and he will testify to that."

"And you showed us the money," the tall boy said to J.B.

There was another long silence.

"So what are you going to do, J.B.?" the heavyset boy said at last.

When J.B. didn't answer, the tall boy made a suggestion: "Maybe you should go tell Snackman and Southgate the truth."

"Or perhaps," said the boy with the shaved head, "you want us to do it?"

J.B. was working his jaw muscles, grinding his molars in anger. Inconspicuously, he balled his hands into fists, then leveled his eyes at Jordan, who unflinchingly returned the gaze.

Finally, J.B. erupted, "I'll think about it," and stormed out of the locker room alone.

It was the week before the Oakwood school district's Christmas vacation was to begin, and Snackman had given his annual Kwanzaa ceremony at the town's elementary, junior high, and high schools. He had just returned to his store and was leaning into the front window, to start setting up the famous Kwanzaa display he installed every year, when he heard the front door creak open and slam shut. Jordan had entered along with the twins. He had picked them up at school and was walking them home.

"That was a *great* Kwanzaa ceremony, Snackman," said Jordan, who was enthusiastically seconded in his opinion by Lisa and Kenny.

"I like the way you use the songs and stories to tell us about the holiday," Lisa added. "You made it so dramatic!"

"And I like what *you* two contributed to the holiday this year," Snackman said to the twins. He reached into the window and pulled out lengths of construction paper the twins had pasted together and painted to resemble a section of kente cloth. It was about three feet long and three inches wide. "I am *so* impressed by your Kwanzaa kente!" Snackman enthused. "Thank you for letting me use it in my Kwanzaa display!"

"When Lisa and I decided to stop fighting over the paints and decided to work together, we decided to design a cloth that stands for the spirit of Kwanzaa," Kenny said proudly. He had recently won a spelling bee with the word *decided.*

"Tell me about it again," Snackman said kindly, his eyes shining in anticipation of what he knew was a well-rehearsed recitation.

"We decided to use the colors of red, green, and black because those are the colors of Kwanzaa," Kenny said. "At the top and bottom of our cloth, we decided to use a pattern that looks like stairs because it means unity and cooperation."

Lisa added, "The shield pattern means that although there

are many obstacles in life, we do not have to let them harm us. And the diamond pattern represents one of the most precious of all the minerals of Africa. It symbolizes the strength and value of black people."

"And last," added Kenny, "we decided to use lots of gold, to symbolize the spiritual wealth of our people." Jordan sidled up to Snackman and quietly thanked him for having faith in him.

"I have faith in all African Americans," Snackman said.

"Even J.B.?" asked Jordan, who hadn't talked to J.B. since the locker room confrontation; J.B. had been avoiding him.

"Even J.B.," said Snackman immediately. "J.B. confessed, and I didn't press charges. I told him to return my money and he did. All except for the sixty dollars he'd spent. In exchange for dropping the charges, J.B. and his parents agreed that he would report to me beginning with a full day of work each day of his Christmas vacation and an afternoon of work each day after school—for the rest of the school year."

"Snackman," Lisa asked, "do you think my grandma will let us celebrate Kwanzaa this year?"

"I don't know, you'll have to ask her," Snackman replied. "But I'll tell you what: If you celebrate, I'll be glad to help."

"*All right!*" yelled Kenny and Lisa simultaneously in voices so loud that everyone in the store stopped what they were doing.

"After all," Snackman added, "we're all in this together."

Two weeks later, on New Year's Eve, the next-to-last day of Kwanzaa, the Garrisons' living room was packed. They were holding their first Kwanzaa Karamu, the Kwanzaa feast, and everyone had come together to celebrate—Jordan's relatives, his late father's friends, his grandmother's friends, his brother and sister's friends and their parents, his friends and their parents, and teachers and neighbors—and Snackman, who was wearing his most resplendent African garb. Later, there would be much laughter, music, dancing, singing, and eating, all through the night; a celebration inspired by the traditions of nations from the four corners of the globe, from everywhere people of African descent lived or had been.

But right now was a solemn moment, and at this solemn moment, Jordan was stuck in the kitchen, alone, unable to part the sea of people to get to the Kwanzaa table. He stayed in the kitchen, and although he was alone there, apart from the heat of the scores of bodies steaming up the living room and dining room of his house, Jordan felt surrounded by love—the love of his family and the love of his friends. He felt embraced in spirit by black people everywhere and throughout all time.

Under Snackman's watchful eye, Jordan's grandmother raised the unity cup, then poured a few drops of water on the carpet, a libation to the ancestors.

"I'd like each of you to think of at least one black person

who has influenced you or meant something to you, but who has passed away," Snackman said. "It doesn't matter whether they are famous or not."

Like waves gently lapping against a sandy shore, a murmur of thanksgiving moved through the house as person after person recited the names of famous African Americans and departed loved ones, one after another. Jordan chose to say the names of his father and mother, and quietly repeated them over and over and over again, like a mantra, like a charm, like an incantation.

Lisa, Kenny, and five other young children lit the seven candles on the kinara and explained the principle of Kwanzaa each represents. It was hard to hear most of what the children said, but all the adults smiled anyway. But when it was Lisa's turn, everyone heard every word. And Kenny's precocious eloquence wowed the party.

At the end of the candle lighting, Snackman pronounced, "You now know the seven principles: *Umoja*/Unity; *Kujichaglia*/Self-Determination; *Ujima*/Collective Work and Responsibility; *Ujamaa*/Cooperative Economics; *Nia*/Purpose; *Kuumba*/Creativity; *Imani*/Faith. Now you can celebrate!"

In the early-morning hours, in the wake of the Karamu, Jordan had a chance to reflect on the year, on the season, and on the day. He was fourteen now and had weathered the first semester of high school. He had lost his father, yet the void from that loss was sometimes filled with something robust and radiant. There were times Jordan could swear that the spirit of his father was in him and guiding him.

At about three o'clock in the morning, after the last Kwanzaa celebrant had bid farewell, Jordan's body and spirit were exhausted, and he felt fatigue slip up behind him like a fog, wrap its soft arms around his shoulders, and draw him toward sleep.

As he crawled into bed and turned out his nightstand lamp, Jordan wondered what had happened to that frayed, stained strip of kente cloth Snackman had given him. He seemed to remember that the twins had last had it. Oh, well, never mind. He would ask them about it tomorrow. But as he started to close his eyes, he caught sight of something in the faint glow of the night-light at the foot of his bed. It was the kente cloth. Jordan switched on his lamp, reached down, and picked up the cloth. To his surprise, the cloth was no longer frayed, singed, stained, or tattered. It looked as if it had been woven anew. And the colors were so vivid that they seemed to give off their own eerie illumination. Jordan stared in disbelief. And then he saw something he hadn't noticed before: In the borders on both ends of the kente were tiny stylized spearheads. Jordan counted. There were seven of them.